First published by Hodder Children's Books in 2004
First U.S. edition, 2004

Printed in China

1 3 5 7 9 10 8 6 4 2

Library of Congress Cataloging-in-Publication Data on file.

Reinforced binding

ISBN 0-7868-5165-1

Visit www.hyperionbooksforchildren.com

For my dear friends, past, present, and future—K.C.
For my friends Mark and Johnny—N.M.

That's What Friends Do

By Kathryn Cave   Illustrated by Nick Maland

HYPERION BOOKS FOR CHILDREN
NEW YORK

Once I was lost
in the woods,
in the woods,

and you
found me.

Once I fell down.
I hurt my knee.
You put your arms around me.

Once I was shy—
I didn't know where to go,
until you saw me.

Once I was slow.
I couldn't catch up.
You waited for me.

Once I was afraid
of the dark, of the dark,
and the creatures that
hide there.

You didn't laugh,
and it wasn't so bad
with you at my side there.

Once I got mad.
I really yelled.
You got mad, too.

When I stopped being mad,
I felt sad and alone.
I thought I'd lost you.

But I hadn't.

"Want to be friends?"

"Okay."

If you are lost
in the woods, in the woods,
I will find you.

If you're afraid
of the cold and the dark,
I'll sit beside you.

I'll wait for you,
I'll share with you,
I'll comfort you,
I'll care for you—
the way you cared for me.

That's what friends do.